COMPLEX CASES
THREE MAJOR MYSTERIES
FOR YOU TO SOLVE

COMPLEX CASES

Three Major Mysteries for You to Solve

JÜRG OBRIST

M

MILLBROOK PRESS

MINNEAPOLIS

First American edition published in 2006 by Millbrook Press, a division of Lerner Publishing Group.

Originally published in Germany by dtv junior
www.dtvjunior.de

Copyright © 2002 by Deutscher Taschenbuch Verlag GmbH & Co. KG, Munich
Translation copyright © 2006 by Jürg Obrist

Millbrook Press
A division of Lerner Publishing Group
241 First Avenue North
Minneapolis, Minnesota 55410 U.S.A.

Website address: www.lernerbooks.com

Library of Congress Cataloging-in-Publication Data

Obrist, Jürg.
    [Klarer Fall?! English]
    Complex cases : three major mysteries for you to solve / by Jürg Obrist.
       p. cm. – (Mini-mysteries)
    Originally published: Munich, Germany : DTV Junior, 2002.
    Summary: The reader can use visual clues and deductive reasoning to help Daisy and Ridley unravel three different crimes.
    ISBN-13: 978-0-7613-3419-4 (lib. bdg. : alk. paper)
    ISBN-10: 0-7613-3419-X (lib. bdg. : alk. paper)
    [1. Detectives--Fiction. 2. Mystery and detective stories.] I. Title. II. Series.
PZ7.O14Com 2006
[Fic]–dc22
                                    2005000008

Manufactured in the United States of America
1 2 3 4 5 6 – BP – 11 10 09 08 07 06

CONTENTS

THE LATEST NEWS FROM DAISY PEPPER AND RIDLEY LONG!

"Hurry, Ridley, a puzzling new case to solve!" Daisy yells through the half-open door. Ridley jumps up, ready for action as always. This time the two detectives will have to concentrate on just one case for several days. The con artists and thieves are getting sneakier, and many problems along the way will have to be solved before they can be caught.

Obviously, Ridley and Daisy are counting on your help. But pay attention! Sometimes you will have to remember clues from earlier in the story. Occasionally you will actually have to turn back a few pages to find the necessary evidence. So be sure to read the stories carefully and to look at the pictures with extra attention. Remember: the law-breakers are getting more and more skilled at what they do!

Daisy and Ridley will solve three difficult cases. They're not expecting any major problems, as long as they have your help!

THE BLUE DIAMOND

In Moosefield's Natural History Museum, preparations are under way for a very special exhibition. Director Henry Toadly has been able to arrange for a first-time-ever show of extremely rare diamonds and other gems. The main attraction will be the biggest and most valuable gem in the world: the Blue Diamond!

At last the show is ready to open. Many famous and distinguished guests have been invited. The excitement increases, because everyone is looking forward to viewing the rare and precious Blue Diamond.

But unfortunately such a special exhibition also attracts some suspicious visitors! Some people attend to do more than admire the sparkling gems—they want to take the Blue Diamond home with them! Plans for taking the rare diamond from the museum are already under way.

STOLEN!!

The grand opening of the show was a big success. The Blue Diamond attracted everybody's attention. People pushed and shoved to get a glimpse of it.

But the next morning—what a shock!—the case is empty. The Blue Diamond has vanished without a trace!

Ridley is reading about the outrageous theft in the *Midday News*. He examines the photograph of last night's opening. "What a fancy crowd!" he exclaims. "Everybody who is anybody was gathered in the museum's hall. And of course Dick Ratzelman was there! But . . . that's strange . . ." Ridley is suddenly perplexed. "Where is Texie Polsch, Dick's female partner? They are usually inseparable at events like this."

Dick is known as a shady character around town. He and Texie run a factory where they manufacture teddy bears. Although no one has ever proven any wrongdoing, there have been rumors that the two are involved in other less-legitimate businesses as well.

Ridley studies the picture closely, but Texie is nowhere to be seen. Daisy, too, becomes curious, "Could it be that they had something to do with the Blue Diamond's disappearance?" she asks, while taking a really good look at the photograph. All of a sudden, she exclaims excitedly, "Bingo! This must be her. Something definitely is fishy and the proof is right here!"

What does Daisy see?

A FEEBLE EXCUSE

Daisy smiles. "On the left side of the photo you can see the leg of a woman who is hiding behind the curtain! Most likely Texie's leg! I'll bet she hid there until everyone left and the museum closed. Then she could easily steal the Blue Diamond!"

Daisy and Ridley explain their theory to Director Toadly. He immediately asks them to investigate the matter further.

Mr. Beesle, the museum's guard, is obviously the person they should question first. But he is not available. He left for vacation just this morning. "Then we might as well begin with Dick and Texie," Ridley reasons.

It doesn't take Ridley and Daisy long to get to Ratzelman's office at the teddy bear factory. "What did you do last night after the museum opening?" they ask Dick and Texie. Dick puffs on his pipe and grins: "As a matter of fact, I had dinner with Director Toadly himself after the museum closed. And then I went straight home. Got there around midnight."

Texie nods her head and adds, "I personally was at the opening only for a short time. I had to leave early to attend the Teddy Bear Convention at the City Center. Afterward, I got home at about 11:30 p.m."

Ridley and Daisy wink at each other. After they leave Ratzelman's office, they agree that Texie's statement can't be true!

Why not?

PROOF!

"We must be on the right track," Ridley says. "Texie could not have been at the Teddy Bear Convention yesterday. According to the poster in Ratzelman's office, the convention is on June twenty-third, and that's actually today."

Daisy, too, is convinced: "They both have something to hide, no question about it. Let's follow them and try to gather some proof."

That same afternoon the two detectives hide in the bushes outside the teddy bear factory. From there they can easily peer into the building's big windows. And they get lucky! They notice Dick and Texie working at the conveyor belt, busily putting heads onto the bears' bodies.

"That's it!" Daisy whispers to Ridley. "Do you see what I see? Now we know for sure that they stole the Blue Diamond!"

What has Daisy discovered?

GETAWAY!

"In the mirror on a locker door, I saw Dick stuff the Blue Diamond into the body of a teddy bear before putting on the head." Daisy explains.

"It's time to grab the two thieves," agrees Ridley.

The two detectives tiptoe around the factory building looking for a secret entrance. They discover an old air vent that is just big enough to squeeze through. They come out in one of the corridors of the factory. Very carefully, they look for Dick and Texie. Ridley and Daisy sneak into a narrow hallway. Through a crack in the wall they finally sight the pair. They are in a small room off to the side, hastily stuffing a suitcase full of teddy bears.

"They're planning on bolting," Ridley whispers. "Did they pack the teddy with the gem inside? We have to get hold of that suitcase to find out." Just then Dick and Texie slip out through a secret door in the wall.

"Darn, they must have noticed us," Daisy says, puzzled.

How were Daisy and Ridley noticed?

THE SECRET TUNNEL

The spotlight in the upper right corner casts shadows on the wall. If you look carefully at the cluttered area, you will notice Daisy's and Ridley's shadows. They are hiding between the ladder and the coat rack. Dick and Texie must have spotted them and taken off.

"This way—they went through this side door," gestures Ridley. The detectives find themselves in a cleverly built secret passageway. "I can hear their footsteps!" Daisy whispers. They move along the tunnel and then suddenly come to a stop. The tunnel branches into two passages.

"Where did they go? Left or right?" Daisy pants breathlessly. For a moment they are stumped. Then Daisy confidently points. "They went this way... Hurry!"

In which direction do they have to go, and why?

A BOAT RIDE TOO LATE!

First Daisy examined Dick's and Texie's footsteps in the tunnel to the right. She noticed that rather than continuing, they actually turned around. The scarf was deliberately placed on the ground to lure the detectives in the wrong direction. The footsteps in the left passage clearly show the direction in which the thieves are running.

Ridley and Daisy follow those tracks until they reach the end of the tunnel. They find themselves at the entrance to the Moosefield Marina.

"I'll bet they swiped a boat. I see that one of them is missing!" Daisy observes. "They'll probably try to get to the lake! Boy, will it be difficult to spot them there among all those other boats."

"Well, at least we can figure out the name or number of the boat they took," Ridley laughs. "That will make our search a little easier."

What is the name or number of the stolen boat?

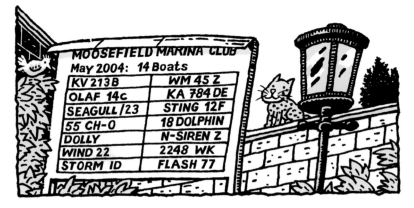

MOOSEFIELD MARINA CLUB
May 2004: 14 Boats

KV 213B	WM 45 Z
OLAF 14c	KA 784 DE
SEAGULL /23	STING 12F
55 CH-O	18 DOLPHIN
DOLLY	N-SIREN Z
WIND 22	2248 WK
STORM ID	FLASH 77

NEW CLUES

According to the marina's list, the number of the missing boat is 2248 WK. Ridley and Daisy dash along the riverbank until they reach the lake. "It must be one of the boats around here!" Daisy guesses. The two detectives stop at a small pier and look for Dick and Texie.

All of a sudden Ridley chuckles: "Told you so. Right over there is our little boat." But there is no trace of Dick and Texie! "Rats! They slipped away again. Let's have a look on board. Maybe we'll find something that will help us get back on their trail."

Carefully Daisy and Ridley sneak onto the deck of the boat and search it thoroughly. "How discouraging . . . not much here," Daisy mutters. Just then she stumbles against a trash can. "What's this?" she wonders, and takes a look at its contents. "Just trash," snorts Ridley, and steps into the cabin. But Daisy carefully inspects the container. After pulling out some old bottles and wrappers, she finds the latest edition of the *Moosefield Echo*, the local newspaper.

Daisy notices that an ad in the corner of the first page was torn off. Then her eyes light on some scraps of paper lying at the bottom of the trash can. She gathers them up and discovers that they have numbers and letters written on them. "Maybe these scraps will give us a fresh clue!" Daisy hopes. "I was always good at puzzles."

What does the message say when the scraps are put back together?

24

THE CHASE INTENSIFIES

When Daisy and Ridley fit the scraps together, they reveal this note: Dora, 278-1306.

"This is definitely a telephone number," Ridley concludes. "But who is Dora?" they both wonder.

"No problem. We'll be able to get that information right over there," says Daisy, pointing to the police station at the corner. They soon find out that Dora is Texie's sister and that she runs a little thrift shop on Beacon Road. "Our next stop!" Daisy exclaims as they both dash off.

Dora is a rather stern-looking woman. She wears strong glasses and mumbles when she talks. Ridley and Daisy ask her if Dick and Texie could possibly be hiding in her store. Dora shakes her head and replies, "They certainly aren't here. True, they did show up a while ago. But when I returned from showing a customer some T-shirts and jeans upstairs, they had disappeared. I still wonder why they came here in the first place."

Daisy and Ridley take a good look around Dora's shop. "Eureka!" shouts Daisy. "They visited you so they could leave something here, something we have been after for quite a while! I hope you don't mind us taking a closer look at it?"

What has Daisy spotted?

26

TEDDY BEARS ALL AROUND

Dick and Texie hid their suitcase in with all the clutter under the staircase. Ridley and Daisy rush to open it. But wouldn't you know—it's empty!

"My goodness," sighs Daisy. "I wonder why... and how... they could have taken all those teddy bears with them? It just doesn't make sense." Daisy stops and again looks around Dora's store. "Wait a second," she says to Dora. "Your sister and Ratzelman left you another present!"

Indeed, scattered among the antiques and collectibles, she notices many Ratzelman Teddys. "Let's gather them all. Perhaps we'll discover the Blue Diamond in one of them. Remember, we only want the genuine Ratzelman Teddys, the ones with the black ribbon in their ears!"

How many Ratzelman Teddys do they find?

DAISY'S EAGLE EYES

"We've found thirteen Ratzelman Teddys and examined each one of them," groans Ridley. And as they had feared, none of them contained the precious stone!

"Naturally, the two scoundrels are long gone, and they took the Blue Diamond with them. I can't imagine how we are ever going to pick up their tracks again," Ridley grumbles as they drag their feet down Beacon Road. Suddenly Daisy stops in front of a newsstand.

"Holy Moly, I get it!" she cries out, her eyes wide. "Look here . . . do you remember?" She points to something, and her thoughts return to the apparently meaningless discovery they made earlier on Dick's and Texie's boat. "I know where we can catch up with the thieves," Daisy proclaims triumphantly.

Where do Daisy and Ridley need to go next?

29

A DUBIOUS DIAMOND DEALER

Daisy's sharp eyes spotted the *Moosefield Echo* at the newsstand. It was the same edition of the newspaper that had been in the trash can on Dick's and Texie's boat. Now it is obvious to her why the ad in the corner was torn off. "*A. Edler. Buy / Sell Diamonds. Piglet's Lane.*" Daisy reads. "That's where we have to look next."

"Sounds good to me," Ridley agrees, "and it's not far off."

Once they get to Piglet's Lane, however, Ridley and Daisy can't find a trace of the diamond dealer. No store, no office, no sign anywhere. "He must not be a respectable dealer if he needs to hide his office so mysteriously," says Daisy dejectedly. But Ridley refuses to give up. He stubbornly continues looking for any clues that would lead them to Edler. And finally, with a twinkle in his eyes, he points and says: "There it is!"

Where is Edler's office?

DICK'S FINAL TRICK

Ridley has spotted Edler's diamond logo in the window of the third floor of the house on the left. Daisy immediately phones Edler's office. She learns from Edler's secretary that Dick and Texie are expected there on Friday at 10:00 A.M.

Ridley and Daisy decide that the time has come to inform Police Officer Kirby. And he agrees to join them when they pay their surprise visit to Edler on Friday morning.

At exactly 10:00 A.M., Officer Kirby waits downstairs, while Daisy and Ridley enter Edler's building. Ridley coughs as they run quickly up the dusty stairs. As they step into Edler's office, they both let out a loud gasp. Texie is at a small table with Edler, happily looking at wedding rings. There is no trace of Dick Ratzelman!

"He did it again . . ." Ridley whispers in frustration. "My coughing must have warned him. So he gave us the slip with the Blue Diamond once again." Texie innocently explains that she has been there alone and claims that Dick is out of town on business. But Daisy giggles knowingly. "We won't have to worry about Ratzelman any more. I know that he was here and that he tried to escape once more. But instead of getting away, he is in Officer Kirby's tight grip at this very moment!"

How does Daisy know that Dick Ratzelman was at Edler's, and how did he try to escape?

CAPTURED AT LAST!

Daisy immediately noticed Dick's lit pipe in Edler's ashtray on the table. He must have fled through the window, as it's still open. In his rush he tipped over the little vase that lies on the chest under the windowsill. Outside, Dick climbed down the vines of ivy that grow along the wall of the building. Tough luck for him, though, since he landed straight in the arms of Officer Kirby.

Dick Ratzelman continues to play innocent. He claims that he knows nothing about the Blue Diamond's whereabouts. "I don't know what you are talking about. Show me proof that I have the gem!" And, in fact, Officer Kirby can't find any trace of the diamond when he searches him.

In the meantime, the detectives who've been keeping an eye on Texie and Edler join Officer Kirby and Dick the Rat. Ridley cheerfully says, "You can arrest them all, Officer. I know where Ratzelman hid the Blue Diamond when he tried to get away!"

Can you spot where Ratzelman hid the gem?

THE SURPRISE ENDING

Of course, Dick did make off with the Blue Diamond. But he quickly hid it in the vines of ivy while he was climbing down. If you look carefully, you can see it among the leaves to the left of the top of the lower window.

Museum Director Toadly should be relieved to finally have the precious Blue Diamond back. But strangely enough, Edler suddenly claims that the stone is actually a fake! "How dare you!" Toadly shouts. "Do you think our museum exhibits phony gems?" But Edler insists. "Look for yourself. Examine the stone, and you will see."

At that moment, a short man in uniform steps forward. It is Mr. Beesle, the museum's guard. He just returned from his vacation this morning. "Excuse me, Director Toadly," he stutters. "I took the liberty of substituting an imitation of the Blue Diamond before I left for vacation. I hid the original gem in a secret place, to make sure it was safe while I was gone. I admit it was a mistake not to inform you about it first, but I had heard rumors of a planned theft."

Dick and Texie are crestfallen. "I just can't believe this. . . ." Dick utters lamely.

To be sure, Ridley and Daisy are also quite astonished: "So all this time we were chasing after a fake!" they laugh together.

"It's time to go!" says Officer Kirby, interrupting the conversation. "The gem was still stolen, phony or not!" And he leads the thieves into the waiting police car.

Can you tell where Mr. Beesle kept the real Blue Diamond?

DOLLY IS MISSING!

Stella Bella, a fortune-teller, and Dolly, her little monkey, are a very special team. Dolly has the extraordinary ability to see into the future. Not only that, she is also able to communicate her visions to Stella, by chattering noisily and gesturing wildly.

Of course, that's the reason why the two of them are so famous everywhere. Many people want Stella to tell their fortunes. But not everyone has innocent intentions, and some of these customers might actually be more interested in stealing the talented little monkey than in having their fortunes told. . . .

BACK TO WORK

Stella is just back from a two-week vacation, and she checks her appointment book. Today, May twelfth, three customers are listed: Stanley Whipple, a night janitor; Wilmer Bozo, an automobile fanatic; and Zilly Rotz, the owner of a hairdressing salon. They each want Stella and Dolly to look into their future.

After their sessions, none of them have any reason to be upset about the predictions. So why does Stanley seem to be a little troubled? First he looks gloomy, and then his face goes pale. Suddenly frightened, Dolly hides somewhere in Stella's mystery-filled room. "I'm sorry, but I don't feel well today," Stanley mutters as he leaves Stella's place. But even afterward, Dolly refuses to come out.

Where does Dolly hide?

SOMETHING IS WRONG!

Dolly is hiding in the right-hand corner of the picture. Her tail, with a bow tied on it, is next to the skeleton.

The next morning, Stella feels that it will be an unlucky day indeed. Usually Dolly jumps onto her shoulder while she brews her coffee. But today the little monkey doesn't jump at all! In fact, she is nowhere to be seen. Stella looks behind the curtains, in the closet—in all of Dolly's favorite hiding places. But Stella is out of luck. Dolly seems to have disappeared. Suddenly Stella gasps as she notices that one of the kitchen windows is open and that the glass is broken! Fearing the worst, she quickly calls Daisy and Ridley.

As soon as the detectives arrive, Stella gives them a full report on all the customers who came the previous day. Ridley and Daisy stick their noses into every corner of her place. Ridley finds a jacket button on the floor. Stella assures them that it's not one of hers. Now there's no doubt in their minds that something is fishy. "Clearly, Dolly did not run away. The little monkey must have been kidnapped last night!" they both conclude.

"I spot three clues, which reveal exactly what happened to Dolly last night!" Ridley exclaims.

What clues has Ridley spotted, and what exactly did happen to Dolly?

THE FIRST SUSPECT: STANLEY WHIPPLE

"It's simple," Ridley and Daisy explain to Stella. "As you can see, during the night someone placed a ladder against the wall of the shed. Then the stranger climbed up to the shed's roof and smashed the kitchen window. The glass pieces lay scattered inside on the windowsill, which proves that it was broken from the outside. After that, the intruder tempted Dolly with a banana. As soon as the monkey was happily munching away, she was grabbed and carried down the ladder. On the way down, Dolly must have tossed the banana peel onto the shed's roof!"

Stella is very upset, and can manage to say only, "Oh, I just hope Dolly is OK!" through her sniffles. Daisy and Ridley promise to do everything they can to get Dolly back. They've concluded that the kidnapper must be one of Stella's three customers from the day before.

"Let's find out what Stanley has to say. He is the only one who seemed upset about Dolly's predictions," Ridley explains.

Stanley Whipple, a widower, lives downtown in a small apartment building. When the detectives ring his doorbell, however, there's no answer. After Daisy rings for the fourth time, she whispers, "It's suspiciously quiet here." She tries to open the door, but it's locked. "It looks as if Mr. Whipple has gone out," Daisy sighs.

But Ridley doesn't agree, "Locked it is, but Stanley must be inside!"

How does Ridley know that Stanley is at home?

44

IS STANLEY REALLY SICK?

Ridley laughs. "Look through the glass door. You can see in the mirror that the key is in the lock. It's locked from the inside, which means that Stanley must be at home!"

Indeed, after several more persistent rings, Stanley finally appears in his bathrobe. "For heaven's sake, can't you see that I'm sick? I have to stay in bed and don't want to be disturbed," he grumbles. But Daisy and Ridley assure him that they only have a couple of questions to ask and then they will be on their way. They follow Stanley into his bedroom and ask him about Dolly's disappearance.

Stanley is somewhat surprised that Dolly is missing. He replies, "Yesterday I felt terribly sick. After my visit to Stella's I went straight to the doctor. He told me I had a high fever and gave me some pills. I went to bed at seven P.M. and haven't left the house since."

Daisy winks at Ridley and answers, "I think Stanley is telling the truth. He must have been in bed all night long."

On the way out, she explains to Ridley why she is so sure.

What makes Daisy so convinced that Stanley is telling the truth, and therefore can't be involved in Dolly's disappearance?

SUSPECT NUMBER TWO: BUT WHERE IS WILMER BOZO?

Daisy noticed Stanley's pill bottle on the night table. There were twelve tablets inside when he got them from the doctor. If Stanley took two tablets every four hours starting at seven P.M., there would be two left by the time Daisy and Ridley arrived. And there are exactly two pills left in the bottle! "Nobody would swallow pills if he weren't sick," Daisy proudly explains.

"So our next candidate is Wilmer," Ridley suggests. They have to ride the bus uptown to Wilmer's home, on the other side of town. When they arrive, they are astounded: What a place! It's more like a junkyard. Rundown shacks, a rotting old barn, and a yard with auto wrecks and engine parts scattered everywhere! "Gee, what a messy place. How can anyone live with so much clutter?"

At first, there is no trace of Wilmer, but after Ridley and Daisy call to him, they hear Wilmer's rough voice. He must be around somewhere, but they still can't see him.

Can you find where Wilmer is?

WILMER'S ALIBI

Wilmer is lying beneath the small truck in the lower left corner, busily fixing the driveshaft. Slowly he crawls out from under, wiping his forehead with his oily hand.

"We would like to ask you some questions," Ridley begins. "Where were you on the night of the twelfth of May?" Wilmer smiles proudly and guides the detectives into his workshop in the old barn. "Well," he clears his throat. "No easier question than that to answer! In the late afternoon I visited Stella Bella to find out what the future holds for me. Then I went straight to—"

"OK, that's just fine! You're off the hook," Ridley suddenly interrupts him. "You have a solid alibi that proves that you didn't have anything to do with the missing monkey!"

What alibi is Ridley talking about?

51

SUSPECT NUMBER THREE: ZILLY THE HAIRDRESSER

Ridley has discovered Wilmer's newest trophy and certificate from the Night Rally in Flintrock. The rally was held on the night of the twelfth to the thirteenth of May. So it would have been impossible for Wilmer to have kidnapped Dolly.

"That leaves Zilly Rotz, Stella's third customer. I could use a visit to a hairstyling salon anyway," Daisy jokes.

When Ridley and Daisy enter the hairdresser's shop, Lola Comb, Zilly's assistant, makes them feel uncomfortable. She is about to trim a customer's greasy mustache. Daisy asks for Mrs. Zilly. But Lola answers, in her surly way, "Mrs. Zilly is gone for the day. I'm working alone here. And aside from this customer, there's nobody else here."

The two detectives take a peek around anyway. "We will pay Mrs. Zilly a visit at her house later," they answer, and quickly leave. They are both quite certain that they are finally on the right track. Ridley and Daisy are convinced that Zilly is actually in the salon, despite Lola's denial.

Why are Daisy and Ridley so certain?

HOT ON THE TRAIL

Thinking back to the Apple Cider Festival, Daisy pictured the small man in her mind. She remembered that he wore a scarf with the initials "E.P." on it. Checking the names on the doorbell, she sees that there is only one name that fits: Erwin Pink.

"Let's wait and see what happens next," Daisy suggests. "They'll have to leave their little nest sometime. And they might lead us directly to Dolly!"

The following afternoon, Zilly and Erwin come out and climb back on the motorbike. "Here we go again, another sweaty chase," Ridley groans. But thank goodness, this time the ride is leisurely and easy. Zilly and Erwin head toward the nearby woods. They park their motorbike and disappear into a rundown cabin. Ridley and Daisy hide close by. From there they can watch the shed and any of the couple's comings and goings.

"I'm sure that they are hiding Dolly in that cabin. The evidence is obvious," Ridley exclaims.

What makes Ridley so sure?

PECULIAR HAPPENINGS AT NIGHT

Among the items behind the cabin Ridley observed a carton full of banana peels. No doubt the remainders of Dolly's feedings!

Zilly and Erwin stay in the shed for the rest of the day. All is quiet. Suddenly, at dusk, they emerge to get back on their motorbike, carrying a large, covered birdcage. Daisy is bursting with excitement. "I bet Dolly is in there!" From a distance they follow the couple, who bring the odd baggage back to Erwin's apartment.

The next morning Ridley and Daisy decide to reveal Dolly's secret whereabouts. Soon Police Officer Kirby joins them. When they ring Erwin's doorbell, they hear quite a commotion from inside the apartment. So it's a big surprise when they enter. There is the birdcage–empty, with the little door wide open!

"Oh dear," Zilly stutters. "Our little birdy, Tipsy, just flew out the window!" But after a quick look around, Ridley laughs. "You mean, Dolly just flew away! It looks as if you wanted the monkey to see into the future of some very specific matters. And to make some quick money for yourselves!"

How does Ridley know that Dolly was in the cage and that she has just escaped?

ESCAPE TO THE BOTANICAL GARDENS

Erwin and Zilly couldn't have had a bird in the cage. The banana peel inside it is a strong clue. And only a monkey would be able to open the little door of the cage. Finally, Ridley has noticed the bow from Dolly's tail on the windowsill.

"Dolly could have fled to the Botanical Gardens nearby," Daisy surmises. "Stella took her there every day. She says it's her favorite place."

Officer Kirby thoughtfully suggests: "It's best to call Stella and ask her to come to the gardens. She's probably the only one who can get Dolly down from the trees."

Shortly afterward, everybody meets in the Botanical Gardens. Stella easily lures Dolly out of hiding.

However, when Officer Kirby accuses Zilly and Erwin of kidnapping Dolly, they become nasty. "You can't accuse us without having any real evidence!" Erwin snorts confidently.

"But of course we have proof!" Ridley laughs. "I almost forgot. We found something in Stella's apartment the morning after the theft. This should do the trick!" Ridley proclaims triumphantly.

What kind of proof do Ridley and Daisy have? And, by the way, where is Dolly hiding in the Botanical Gardens?

WATCH OUT, RIDLEY!

At the beginning of this case, Ridley found a button in Stella's apartment. It's the one missing from Erwin's jacket. This is clear evidence that Erwin, most likely with Zilly's help, kidnapped Dolly.

Where did the monkey hide in the Botanical Gardens? In the bush right next to Daisy.

Naturally, when Stella appeared, Dolly jumped right into her arms. Stella was overjoyed to have her little fortune-teller back again. And to show her appreciation, she offers Ridley and Daisy a special look into their future.

"For Daisy everything looks fine . . ." she announces happily. But for Ridley, she and Dolly see some odd events ahead. "Be particularly careful," she advises him. "Soon there will be a rather painful occurrence. And you will feel it for quite some time!"

"Yeah, right!" Ridley laughs skeptically as he and Daisy leave. He doesn't believe in fortune-telling at all. . . . But perhaps he should reconsider?

THE KIDNAPPING OF ROBBY BOB

Professor Kleinstein is about to announce a major breakthrough. Together with his colleague Tripplitz, he has created "Robby Bob," a very special robot! Once programmed, the intelligent machine is able to do just about everything humans can do. Once their final tests on Robby Bob's "brain," his central controls, have been completed, the two professors plan to unveil the remarkable robot to the scientific community.

However, the underground world is also buzzing with excitement about this amazing invention. What a great tool it would make for the business of stealing and swindling!

One gang in particular is already planning how to get their hands on Robby Bob. Ridley and Daisy call Professor Kleinstein to advise him about this serious threat.

THE CROOKS GET NOSY

Professor Kleinstein is sitting with Daisy and Ridley in his laboratory. They are discussing the precautions to be taken to prevent Robby Bob from being stolen. Daisy and Ridley have top-secret information that Peck Sleeze and his gang are after the robot.

"Those thieves are itching to get their hands on Robby Bob!" Ridley warns.

So Professor Kleinstein suggests that his colleague Professor Tripplitz take the robot to a secret place. "It's the only way to secure it," he explains.

Minutes later Professor Tripplitz is on his way to pick up Robby Bob. "We will perform the last tests on the robot's brain in an undisclosed location," Kleinstein explains.

"Very good," Ridley agrees. "There is no beating about the bush where Peck Sleeze is concerned. When he wants something, he doesn't stop at anything to get it."

If Ridley only knew how right he is! He and the others haven't noticed, but one of Sleeze's gang is spying on them at this very moment.

Which one of Sleeze's gang, shown in the mug shots, is shadowing them?

Tony Glurp

Mirta Bacon

Roley Poley

ROBBY BOB TAKES A RIDE

Tony Glurp sits in the tree outside the lab and watches through his binoculars. He has a bandage on his cheek.

In the meantime, Professor Tripplitz has arrived to take Robby Bob to the new location. Too bad for Tony! Because he is so determined to find a way to get into the lab, he misses seeing the robot being taken away!

In the evening, while Professor Kleinstein is busy with some work, his fax machine rings in the room next door. He quickly leaves to get the message.

When Kleinstein returns, has something changed? What would prove that Tony was sneaking around Kleinstein's laboratory?

THE PLOT THICKENS

Yes! Tony has already managed to get into Kleinstein's lab. The intruder shifted the chair in front of the computer a bit while nosing around. But unfortunately the distracted professor doesn't notice it.

Tony hides in Kleinstein's lab and waits until the professor goes into the kitchen to cook an omelet for dinner. Then Tony snoops around, looking for a clue that would lead him to Robby Bob.

"Nothing at all," Tony mutters in frustration. But just then he discovers the fax message that came in earlier.

The weird signs on the paper confuse Tony. No wonder! It's a message from Tripplitz in a secret code. The two professors have agreed to write everything in code for security reasons.

Tony decides to crack the code later, and stuffs the paper in his pocket. But in fact, he could have made his job a lot easier. All he had to do was look a bit closer at the mess on the professor's desk.

Can you decode the secret message?

ROBBY BOB IN DANGER

The professor left the key to the code on his desk. The alphabet has twenty-six lettters. Therefore 1 = A, 2 = B, and so on. All you have to do is replace the sign with the letter equivalent to it in the message. It then reads:

DEAR KLEINSTEIN
EVERYTHING IS READY FOR THE TEST! WE
BEGIN NEXT FRIDAY IN THE GENERATOR
FACTORY STEAM AND CO. HALL C.
GREETINGS
TRIPPLITZ

Early the next morning Professor Kleinstein finally notices that the fax message is missing. He calls Daisy and Ridley immediately and shouts into the telephone: "It's happened! Those thieves have gotten hold of Tripplitz's secret message. If they manage to decode it, they will soon get Robby Bob!" Between groans, he reads the message to the detectives.

"Holy smokes!" Ridley yells. "We're on our way to the generator factory now."

"I'll notify Tripplitz, and then meet you there," Kleinstein answers, trying to stay calm.

Shortly afterward, Ridley and Daisy arrive at the factory. They immediately rush to the janitor to question him. But if they had looked around first, they would know that Peck Sleeze and his crew have already cracked the code. In fact, they are already on the job!

Can you discover why that is?

THE DUPED JANITOR

If you examine the pizza van parked outside the factory you will find that the word "PIZZA" is painted over the name "PECK SLEEZE." So in fact Sleeze's crew must already be there, ready to steal Robby Bob.

Ridley asks the janitor if there have been any strange people trying to get into the factory. But he shakes his head and replies, "Nothing unusual today... except a Professor Tripplitz arrived and said that he had an appointment with the construction office. I figure that's where he went!"

Just at that moment, Professor Tripplitz hastily approaches them from across the street. "Professor Kleinstein called me," he bellows. "These miserable swindlers have—"

"Professor Tripplitz," sputters Daisy, astonished. "We were just told that you're already in the factory." It's obvious that someone has pretended to be Professor Tripplitz in order to get into the factory to find Robby Bob!

Suddenly Daisy yells, "Quick! We have to hurry to Hall C. We may be too late!" She has just noticed something inside the janitor's station that has made her suspect the worst.

What has Daisy discovered?

HOODWINKED!

"On the keyboard hanging inside the janitor's station, the key to Hall C is missing. The fake Professor Tripplitz must have reached through the open window and grabbed it!" Daisy explains as they rush into the factory.

All is quiet in Hall C. But obviously someone has just been there and left a big mess. "Dash it, Robby Bob is gone!" Tripplitz moans.

Ridley angrily adds, "The thief took what he wanted and got away."

At this moment Professor Kleinstein arrives. "If that gang figures out how Robby Bob's central controls work, it will be very bad. I hate to think what they could do with the robot!" he sighs.

Daisy is busy looking for clues. "Maybe the thief is still in the building," she suggests hopefully. "He can't have much of a lead since we got here so quickly."

"He could have tried to get away through that door over there. But he wouldn't get far, because it only opens into the factory's rear courtyard," Ridley figures.

As they hurry to investigate, Kleinstein suddenly says, "I think that this is a trap to lead us in the wrong direction. The thief is probably making his getaway at this very moment."

Is Professor Kleinstein right in his suspicion?

PREPARING FOR A TRIP

In fact, the thief was still in the hall when his pursuers arrived. After he snatched Robby Bob, he hid behind a huge box. While they were examining the door to the rear courtyard, he dashed up the stairs and slipped through door C in the upper right corner of the hall. You can spot his shoe near the door.

Ridley, Daisy, and the professors rush to the windows, where they see the speeding pizza van pull away. "So Peck Sleeze and his gang kidnapped Robby Bob!" Ridley exclaims.

The detectives lose no time, and quickly arrive at Peck's house. They watch Peck's crew load the pizza van with various boxes and packages. "I bet they're preparing to sneak away with Robby Bob," Daisy whispers.

"Definitely," Ridley agrees. "Do you notice that all the stuff they're carrying out is labeled with the same sign, 'MOLOCH.' I wonder what that means?"

Daisy grins. "Get ready for a trip! I've just figured it out!"

What does MOLOCH mean?

LOST TRACKS

Daisy noticed that Roley Poley put a road map of Castle Moloch into the van. The castle is located several miles to the north.

Daisy quickly gets her motorbike. When she returns, Peck Sleeze and his helpers are just about to drive off in the van. Daisy and Ridley tail them on the motorbike at a safe distance.

The ride through the countryside goes smoothly. Daisy keeps a close eye on the van. But then the traffic begins to get heavier and heavier. Shortly after they pass the town of Lovell, there's a sharp curve and Sleeze's van suddenly vanishes. There's no trace of it at all! Daisy and Ridley are frantic and helpless all at once. "Darn it, they got away!" Daisy shouts. "How can we ever catch up with them again?" They have no choice but to continue and hope to spot the van.

After half a mile or so, Daisy perks up. "I think we're OK. There is an intersection with signs ahead!" But when she wants to continue toward Castle Moloch, Ridley insists they stop for a moment. "Something is fishy here," he suspects. "I have the feeling they noticed us following them. This street sign can't be right. It's been tampered with, for sure!"

Why does Ridley come to this conclusion, and which road do they have to take?

PECK SLEEZE'S LAIR

Ridley is right! He and Daisy have already passed through the town of Lovell. Therefore they would be coming from there and not from Westlo. Peck's gang turned the street sign clockwise. So the road to the right, in fact, goes to Westlo and the road to the left to Castle Moloch! Ridley and Daisy now proceed in the right direction.

Finally they are able to make out the striking silhouette of Castle Moloch on the horizon. When they pull up to the main gate, Daisy exclaims, "What a ramshackle old castle. It's practically falling down."

"It looks deserted. Could Peck and his crew really use this place as their hideaway?" Ridley whispers.

"No doubt about that," Daisy laughs. "In fact, they've just recently arrived. There is the proof!"

What proof is Daisy referring to?

INSIDE CASTLE MOLOCH

Daisy points to the cigarette butt on the left side of the path near the entrance gate. "It's still smoldering, so they must have come through here just a little while ago," she murmurs.

Ridley agrees, and the two detectives sneak down the path toward the entrance to the castle. From inside they hear hasty footsteps. Then a door slams shut and a key is turned in a lock. After that, all is quiet again. "Strange," Ridley says softly. He presses his ear to the rough wooden door. "There's nothing else! Total silence!"

Ridley cautiously pulls the door handle. It's unlocked. He slowly opens the heavy door so they can slip inside. Ridley and Daisy find themselves in a gloomy, dusty hallway. On either side there are many doors leading to other rooms. "How are we going to find the crooks with all these doors everywhere?" Ridley wonders.

Cool as a cucumber, Daisy replies, "I'm afraid we'll just have to check out every single room behind these doors."

"Maybe not," Ridley suddenly laughs. "I think I know which door we should look behind."

Which door is Ridley referring to, and how does he know?

AMONG THE CROOKS

"When we listened from the outside before, there was a sound of footsteps, a door slamming, and finally a key turning. This means that a door got closed and was locked afterwards," Ridley remembers. "Except for the little door on the right, all the others are slightly open. So the gang should be in the room behind that closed door."

Thanks to their excellent detective training, Daisy and Ridley have no trouble opening the locked door, especially because it is old and brittle! Ridley and Daisy sneak into the room and climb up a narrow staircase. They know they are on the right track, because they hear voices in the distance. Carefully, they make their way into an anteroom. Behind a crumbling stone wall, they watch Tony Glurp and Mirta Bacon carrying big boxes and barrels into the nearby laboratory.

In the lab, Peck Sleeze and Roley Poley are bent over plans spread out on a table. Robby Bob stands in the back, about to go through the final tests. "This is it," Daisy whispers to Ridley. "We have to act now, before they figure out how to use the robot."

"And what exactly do you propose?" Ridley asks, frustrated.

Daisy gives him a wink: "I have a plan!" And Daisy is soon in the midst of the thieves.

How did Daisy manage to get into the lab?

DAISY'S INGENIOUS TRICK

In the anteroom, Daisy quickly jumped into the empty box marked 7 and pulled down the lid. Tony and Mirta, figuring that the box was filled with material, unknowingly carried Daisy into the lab.

But now for the hard part! How to get to Robby Bob's central controls and change its program! Luckily Peck Sleeze and Roley Poley are still at the table studying the plans. Daisy quickly slips behind their backs to get to the robot.

Daisy thinks back to Professor Kleinstein's explanation of Robby Bob's "brain." She remembers the emergency command the professor told her about. So she grips the little handle on the switchboard of the control center and begins at the "start" sign. It has to pass the appropriate single letters in the right order. The process should result in the full command sentence by the time the handle arrives at the "finish" sign. Daisy anxiously hopes to place the command successfully. If she does, Robby Bob will then activate and execute it instantly, once turned on by the thieves.

What is the emergency command? Be aware there are some letters on the switchboard that have nothing to do with the command!

ROBBY BOB THE HERO

"Done! Now it just has to work," Daisy wishes desperately. The command sentence she programmed is:

ALARM STAGE ONE INSTANT LOCKUP

Silently she sneaks unnoticed out of the lab. Daisy and Ridley immediately rush out to notify the professors and Officer Kirby. It is their hope that once Robby Bob gets up and running, the crooks will be in their hands!

They use the telephone in a nearby diner. While they wait, they each enjoy a steaming cup of hot chocolate.

When the professors, Officer Kirby, and the police arrive, Daisy fills them in on all that's happened. "I am so anxious to know if the command worked! Let's get going." They cautiously approach Castle Moloch. It's strangely quiet when they enter the ruins. But the minute they mount the stairs they are joyfully greeted by Robby Bob. The robot rolls, somewhat shakily, toward them. It is waving the key to the laboratory, peeping and squeaking like a bird. Peck and his gang are trapped in the lab and angrily pounding at the locked iron gate. Robby Bob did exactly as programmed—locked them up!.

But Professor Kleinstein and Professor Tripplitz still don't look very happy. They are muttering something about idiots, and fussing with Robby Bob's feet.

Why are they so annoyed?

ABOUT THE AUTHOR/ ARTIST

Jürg Obrist studied photography at the Arts and Crafts School in Zurich, Switzerland. He then moved to the United States, where he lived for many years. At the moment he is back in Zurich with his family, doing freelance illustration and writing articles for teen magazines.

The author originally wrote this book in German, but his years in the United States perfected his English to the point that he was also able to be the translator for this edition. The job was a particular challenge because the words in the artwork had to be translated—but no problem. Jürg is also the illustrator of the original edition, so he was able to redo the calligraphy as well.

This is the third in a series of three mini-mystery books, all of which have been very popular with young would-be detectives in Germany as well as in France and South Korea. The other books in the series are *Case Closed: Forty Mini-Mysteries for You to Solve* and *Open and Shut Cases: 40 More Mini-Mysteries for You to Solve*.

Match your wits against Daisy and Ridley
in these other books by Jürg Obrist:

CASE CLOSED

40 Mini-Mysteries for You to Solve

OPEN AND SHUT CASES

40 More Mini-Mysteries for You to Solve